D0419321

a gift for us to share

to:
....

from:
....

OTHER HELEN EXLEY GIFTBOOKS:

Smile

The Littlest Teddy Bear Book

Giggles: A Joke Book

To a Very Special Mother

The Love between Mothers and Daughters

The Love between Mothers and Sons

To Pam, All My Love, Jane x
To Marion, my mom. Just to say that every word in this book is true.
With all my love, Helen x

Published in 2005 by Helen Exley Giftbooks in Great Britain,
and Helen Exley Giftbooks LLC in the USA.

12 11 10 9 8 7 6 5 4 3 2

Illustrations © Jane Massey 2005
Copyright © Helen Exley 2005
The moral right of the author has been asserted.

ISBN 1-905130-39-2

A copy of the CIP data is available from the British Library on request.

Printed in China

Helen Exley Giftbooks, 16 Chalk Hill, Watford, Herts WD19 4BG, UK,
Helen Exley Giftbooks LLC, 185 Main Street, Spencer MA 01562, USA.
www.helenexleygiftbooks.com

Written by Helen Exley and Illustrated by Jane Massey

Me
and my
Mum

This is my Mum.

She is really fun.

She sings and dances with me.

Jumping, thumping, laughing...

We make a lot of noise.

My Mum's hands

are really kind and gentle.

When I hurt my arm she mended me

and teddy too.

She looks after everyone.

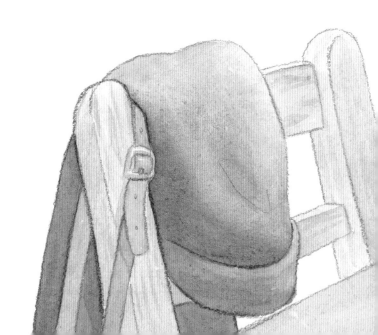

My Mum has to work so that
we can buy things. I don't know how
she doesn't get driven mad
by the computer, the homework,
the phone, ME!

She really loves me, you know.

Sometimes my Mum is naughty.

When we go shopping she says

"My feet are killing me!"

So we take off our shoes

and put our feet in the fountain.

"Ahh," she says, "that's better."

One day my Mum was very tired.

She said, "I've had quite enough!"

So I tucked her in

and gave her some peace and quiet.

My Mum protects me.

She helps me not to fall off my bike

(and do other dangerous, silly things!).

She would stop anyone else

from hurting me. She is very brave

and makes me brave too.

My Mum is always busy –
she has too much to do. Washing, rushing,
cooking, tidying my toys.
It never stops.
Poor Mum!

I give my Mum lessons.

She is really useless because she can't kick

and she can't catch.

I tell her, "Keep trying Mum,

I love you anyway."

My Mum is a softie.

When we sit on the sofa

and watch her old movies she cries.

We cry together.

My Mum is kind. We work together on my reading and my sums. If I really, really try she gives me a star, even when I get them wrong!

One night I had a bad dream.

The scary crocodiles and lions

were coming to get me.

Mum hugged me and read me to sleep.

When she is there I always feel safe.

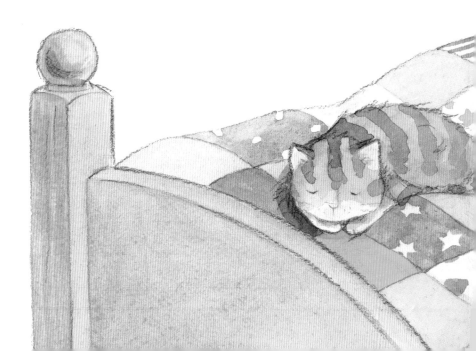

My Mum has special times for me.
No matter how busy she is, we do
our own thing. Just me and my Mum.
Reading, dancing, laughing,
going off together...
This is my really special Mum.

WHAT IS A HELEN EXLEY GIFTBOOK?

Helen Exley Giftbooks cover the most powerful of all human relationships:
the bonds within families and between friends, and the theme of personal values.
No expense is spared in making sure that each book is as meaningful
a gift as it is possible to create: good to give, good to receive.
You have the result in your hands. If you have loved it – tell others!
There is no power on earth like the word-of-mouth recommendation of friends!